Stories From The PANCHATANTRA

SPIDER BOOKS

Stories From The Panchatantra
ISBN 81- 88759 - 00 - 7

Published by
SPIDER BOOKS
AH-73/1, 7th Main Road, Shanthi Colony
Anna Nagar, CHENNAI - 600 040 (INDIA)
Email: spiderbooks@dishnetdsl.net
Phone: 044-52171048

Retold by
Jyotsna Bharti

Illustrations
Venkatesh

Printed in India

CONTENTS

CONTENTS

The Ugly Tree

Long, long ago, in a dense forest there were thousands of tall and beautiful trees. They were happy, but proud of themselves. Among them there also was an ugly tree whose branches were badly twisted. Its roots had uneven curves. All the trees made fun of the ugly tree.

"How are you, hunchback?" the other trees always shouted and their laughter made the ugly tree feel sad. But he never raised a voice against them. The ugly tree thought, "I wish I were as beautiful as the other trees. Why did God do this to me? Neither can I provide shade to the travellers nor can the birds make their nests on me. Nobody needs me."

One day, a woodcutter came to the forest. He took a look at the trees and said, "These trees are lovely. I must cut them." As soon as he picked up his axe the trees became frightened.

'Chop, chop, chop' went the woodcutter's axe and one by one the trees started to fall. "None of us is going to be spared," screamed one of the beautiful trees. Soon he too was brought to ground by the woodcutter's axe.

By now the woodcutter had come near the ugly tree. He had just raised his axe when suddenly he noticed how crooked the tree was. "Hmm! This crooked tree seems to be useless for me. I cannot make long straight logs of this tree," he thought. And he moved towards another beautiful tree.

The ugly tree heaved a huge sigh of relief. He realised that by making him ugly, God had actually given him a boon.

From that day the ugly tree never complained. He was happy with his crooked branches. He never forgot how he was spared from the woodcutter's axe, only because he was ugly.

The Golden Swan

Long time ago, there lived a King. He was lazy and liked all the comforts of life. He never carried out his duties as a King. "Our King does not take care of our needs. He also ignores the affairs of his kingdom," the people complained.

One day, the King went into the forest to hunt. After having wandered for quite sometime, he became thirsty. To his relief, he spotted a lake. As he was drinking water, he suddenly saw a golden swan come out of the lake and perch on a stone. "A golden swan. I must capture it," thought the King.

But as soon as he held his bow up, the swan disappeared. And the King heard a voice, "I am the golden swan. If you want to capture me you must come to heaven."

Surprised, the King said, "Please show me the way to heaven." "Do good deeds, serve your people and the messenger from heaven would come to fetch you," replied the voice.

The selfish King, eager to capture the swan, tried doing some good in his kingdom. "Now, I suppose a messenger will come to take me to heaven," he thought. But no messenger came.

The King then disguised himself and went out into the street. There he tried helping an old man. But the old man became angry and said, "You need not try to help. I am in this miserable state because of our selfish King. He has done nothing for his people."

Suddenly, the King heard the golden swan's voice, "Do good deeds and you will come to heaven." It dawned on the King that by doing selfish acts he will not go to heaven.

He realised that his people needed him and carrying out his duties was the only way to heaven. After that day he became a responsible King.

The Rightful Owner

Once upon a time, there lived a farmer named Gopal. He had a cow which gave lots of milk. Gopal had grown quite rich, selling the milk.

One day, the cow fell ill and stopped giving milk. Thinking she would never recover, Gopal drove her out of his house. "Now my owner does not need me. I will never return to him," thought the sad cow and ran away.

On the way, the hungry cow fell unconscious. Dharma, a kind-hearted farmer noticed her and brought her to his house.

After a few days the cow recovered. Dharma thought, "I wonder who this cow belongs to." But he was unable to find the owner. Soon, the cow gave birth to a calf and started giving milk again. Dharma fed her well and looked after the calf, too. By selling the cow's milk Dharma became a

wealthy man. Everyone wanted to buy Dharma's cow's milk. The cow's fame spread everywhere.

Gopal too came to know about it. "I wonder if that cow is the same one I had driven away," thought Gopal. When Gopal went to Dharma's house, he found that it was indeed his cow. "That cow belongs to me," said Gopal. But Dharma refused to return the cow.

"I will take the help of the Village Panchayat," shouted Gopal. And the next day, the Village Panchayat heard the case. "Let the cow decide for herself who she wants to live with," said the Panchayat Head.

So the cow was placed between Dharma and Gopal. The cow walked away from Gopal and started licking Dharma's hand. She knew the difference between Gopal's selfishness and Dharma's kindness. The Panchayat handed over the cow to her rightful owner, Dharma.

The Judge Monkey

Once two cats were passing through a street. Suddenly they spotted a loaf of bread lying beneath a tree. Both pounced upon it and caught the loaf at the same time. "It's mine. I saw it first," claimed one cat. While the other said, "I pounced upon it first and so it belongs to me." After having fought for a while, one cat said, "Let us divide it into two and take one piece each." "Indeed, a good idea," said the other cat, "But how do we divide it now?"

A monkey sitting on the branch of the tree had watched all that happened between the two cats. "That loaf of bread looks good. I could do with it myself," he thought. Slowly he came down from the tree and walked up to the confused cats.

"Yes, my dear friends! Can I help you?" asked the monkey. The cats told him what the problem was and said, "Why don't you be the judge between us?" When the

monkey nodded, the cats said, "Please divide this loaf for us."

The clever monkey smilingly broke the bread into two pieces. But one piece was a little bigger than the other. "Oh no! I will take a little bite of this piece to make both equal," said the monkey, slyly. He took a bite from the bigger piece. But he had taken a big bite. "Uh oh! Now it has become smaller than the other piece. I will just have to take a little bite from this piece now," said the monkey.

He took another bite. The two cats sat in front of the monkey, seeing the loaf of bread they had found getting smaller and smaller. When the whole loaf was eaten, the monkey said, "I am sorry. It was really difficult dividing that loaf. I must be going now." And the monkey jumped onto the tree and was gone. "If only we had not quarrelled among ourselves, we need not have to go hungry now," said the two cats.

Pigeons' Hospitality

Once upon a time, there lived two pigeons. They were husband and wife. They spent their day looking for food. In the evening they would come and rest on their favourite tree in the forest.

One evening, the wife returned home early. As usual she was waiting for her husband, when suddenly it started raining. She started to worry. "Where are you, dear! You never get so late," she whispered to herself.

Just then she saw a bird-catcher coming towards her. In a cage he had a pigeon. It was her husband. "Oh no, what shall I do now? I wish I can help my husband," she said. She desperately tried to distract the bird-catcher by flapping her wings, but all in vain.

Soon it stopped raining, "Brrr! It's so cold," said the bird-catcher. His clothes were

wet. He decided to sit under the same tree where the two pigeons lived.

The poor wife sat by her husband's cage and started to cry. The husband said, "Don't feel sad, dear. We now have a guest. This man is shivering and hungry. He needs your help."

Hearing this, the wife flew around getting dry twigs. She made a fire for the bird-catcher. Then she looked at the bird-catcher and said, "You are our guest, since I have no food to offer, I'll jump into this fire. You can eat me."

By now the bird-catcher was overwhelmed by the hospitality of the humble pigeon couple. He at once stopped the wife from jumping into the fire.

He opened the cage and set the husband free. "I have been cruel and selfish. I will never trap any bird in my net again," said the bird-catcher and went away. The two pigeons were happy to be reunited.

The Bonded Donkey

In a small village, there lived a potter. He had a donkey. Everyday his donkey would carry soil from the field to his house. Since the field was quite far off, the potter would rest under a tree midway, tying his donkey nearby.

One day, the potter forgot to take the rope with which he tied the donkey everyday. When they reached the tree, he thought, "How do I tie this donkey today? He might run away if I sleep." The potter decided to lie down holding the donkey's ears so that the donkey wouldn't run away.

But this way neither the donkey was comfortable nor the potter was able to rest. A saint, who happened to be passing by, saw the potter holding on to the donkey's ears. When the potter told him what the problem was, the wise saint said, "Take the donkey to the place where you tie him everyday. Pretend to tie him using an imaginary rope.

I assure you he won't run away." The potter did what the saint had said.

He left the donkey and went to take a nap. When he woke up, to his surprise and relief, he found the donkey standing in the same place.

Soon the potter prepared to leave for home. But the donkey did not move. "What is wrong with this donkey!" exclaimed the potter in frustration.

Luckily, the potter saw the wise saint again. He ran up to the saint and told him about the donkey's strange behaviour.

The saint said, "You tied up the donkey but did you untie him? Go and pretend to untie the rope." The potter followed the saint's advice.

Now the donkey was ready to leave for home. The potter thanked the wise saint and went home happily with his donkey.

The Foolish Fish

In a huge pond, there lived many fish. They were arrogant and never listened to anyone. In this pond, there also lived a kind-hearted crocodile.

He advised the fish, "It does not pay to be arrogant and overconfident. It could be your downfall." But the fish never listened to him. "There is that crocodile, advising us again," they would say.

One afternoon, the crocodile was resting beside a stone near the pond, when two fishermen stopped there to drink water.

The fishermen noticed that the pond had many fish. "Look! This pond is full of fish. Let's come here tomorrow with our fishing net," said one of them. "I am surprised we have not seen this place before!" exclaimed the other.

The crocodile heard all this. When the fishermen left, he slowly slipped into the

pond and went straight to the fish. "You all better leave this pond before dawn. Early morning those two fishermen are going to come with their net," warned the crocodile.

But the fish just laughed and said, "There have been many fishermen who have tried to catch us. These two are not going to catch us either. Don't you worry about us, Mr. Crocodile," they said in a mocking voice.

The next morning, the fishermen came and threw their net in the pond. The nets were big and strong. Very soon all the fish were caught.

"If only we had listened to Mr. Crocodile. He had only wanted to help. For our arrogance we have to pay with our lives," said the fish.

The fishermen took the fish to the market and sold them for a good profit.

Long ago, a poor brahmin lived with his family in a small house. His disciples would help him with food and clothes. He somehow managed to pass his days.

One day, the brahmin received two calves as a gift from one of his disciples. He was overjoyed. Though he had difficulty in arranging for fodder and grain for the calves, he managed to feed the two calves. Years passed by and the calves grew up into two strong bullocks.

A thief had seen the bullocks. "The foolish brahmin doesn't even know the proper use of those bullocks. I will steal the bullocks and sell them," he thought.

That evening, the thief started for the brahmin's house. While on his way, the thief was stopped by a fierce demon. "I am hungry. I will eat you," said the demon, in a thundering voice. "Wait! Wait, dear

friend! I am a thief. I am on my way to the brahmin's house to steal his bullocks. You can eat the brahmin instead of me," said the thief.

The demon agreed. The thief and the demon proceeded towards the brahmin's house. Reaching the house the thief said, "Let me take the bullocks and go. Then you can eat the brahmin." "No! Let me eat the brahmin first. I am hungry," roared the demon. The two started to quarrel.

The noise woke up the brahmin. As soon as he saw the demon he started chanting some mantras. The demon uttered a sharp cry, "AAIEE!" and disappeared.

Then the brahmin got hold of a thick stick, "You tried to steal my bullocks, did you?" said the brahmin. And he thrashed the thief. Thus the brahmin saved himself from the demon.

The Clever Crow

Once upon a time, there lived a crow. She had built her nest on a tree. At the root of the same tree, a snake had made its home.

Whenever the crow laid eggs, the snake would eat them up. The crow felt helpless, "That evil snake. I must do something. Let me go and talk to him," thought the crow.

The next morning, the crow went to the snake and said politely, "Please spare my eggs, dear friend. Let us live like good neighbours and not disturb each other." "Huh! You cannot expect me to go hungry. Eggs are what I eat," replied the snake, in a nasty tone. The crow felt angry and she thought, "I must teach that snake a lesson."

The next day, the crow was flying over the king's palace. She saw the princess wearing an expensive necklace. Suddenly a thought flashed in her mind and she swooped down, picked up the necklace in her beak and flew off to her nest.

When the princess saw the crow flying off with her necklace, she screamed, "Somebody help, the crow has taken my necklace."

Soon the palace guards were running around in search of the necklace. Within a short time the guards found the crow. She still sat with the necklace hanging from her beak.

The clever crow thought, "Now is the time to act." And she dropped the necklace, which fell right into the snake's pit.

When the snake heard the noise, it came out of its hole. The palace guards saw the snake. "A snake! Kill it!" they said. With big sticks they beat the snake and killed it.

Then the guards took the necklace and went back to the princess. The crow was happy, "Now my eggs will be safe," she thought.

Thousands of years ago, there lived a King. His people loved him since he looked after their needs well. At the end of every month he would invite some noblemen of his kingdom to analyse his work and advise him.

The King built many things. Every year he would rebuild his palace and every time it looked better than before. "Marvellous! Unmatched!" the courtiers would praise and the King would feel elated.

One day the King thought, "This year, I will build the perfect palace, with all comforts. It should be praised not only within my kingdom but also by the people of the neighbouring states."

The next day, the King worked out a perfect design for his perfect palace. After finalising it, he handed it over to the builders and masons. In about a month, the perfect palace of the King's dream was

ready. The King invited noblemen of his kingdom, as well as the neighbouring states, to get their opinion about the palace.

"Unbelievable! Indeed, it's a perfect palace," cheered the noblemen in unison. But a saint standing in the corner was silent.

The King wondered why the saint was silent, when everyone was praising his palace. He walked up to the saint and said, "Please tell me, O Saint, why you are silent. Isn't my palace perfect?"

The saint replied in a calm voice, "Dear King! Your palace is strong and will last forever. It is beautiful but not perfect, since the people living in it are mortals. They are not permanent. Your palace will live forever but not the people in it. That is why I am silent. Man is born with empty hands and so does he die."

The King thanked the saint for his wise words and never tried to build a perfect palace again.

The Holy Snake

Long ago, in a small village lived Vishnudutta, a poor brahmin farmer. He worked hard but was not able to earn much. His son, Somadutta was always asking for more money. "Be satisfied with what you have, my son," Vishnudutta would say.

One day, Vishnudutta was resting in his field after work. Suddenly, he noticed a snake on the nearby mound. On seeing Vishnudutta, the snake coiled and sat up with a raised hood. "It looks so calm and peaceful. May be it is a deity," thought Vishnudutta. He brought a bowl of milk from his house and offered it to the snake.

Next morning, when Vishnudutta came to collect the bowl, he found a gold coin in it. "I am sure this is a holy snake," he thought. After that it became a regular practice for him to offer prayers and milk to the snake. And every morning he got a

gold coin in the bowl near the mound. This made Vishnudutta a rich man.

Once, while Vishnudutta was away, his son Somadutta had to keep the bowl of milk near the snake. He thought, "I guess there is a treasure of gold coins beneath this mound. If I can kill this snake and dig under the mound I'll get all the gold!" With gold on his mind, Somadutta, tried to kill the snake. The snake bit Somadutta and managed to escape.

When Vishnudutta returned, his wife told him everything. "I always warned you against greed," said Vishnudutta to his son. Then he ran towards the holy snake. With folded hands he asked for forgiveness and offered milk.

But this time the snake did not accept it. "I spared your son's life because of your kindness. But you will have to pay for his greed. I shall not help you any more," said the snake and disappeared.

The Ungrateful Lion

In a dense forest, lived a fierce lion. He was very cruel. One day the lion was caught in a hunter's trap. One by one many animals passed by. "Please help me!" pleaded the lion. But none of the animals listened to his pleas.

After a while, a man happened to come into the forest. He saw the lion. The lion said, "I will die of hunger and suffocation. Please help me out, O kind man." The man was thoughtful. "I assure you I will never harm you. Please help me now. The hunter will be here anytime now," said the lion.

The man felt sorry for the lion and set the beast free. As soon as the lion was free, he let out a fierce roar. "I have been trapped in the cage for a long time. I am hungry. I will have to eat you," said the lion, looking at the man. "But you promised that you would not harm me," said the man, in a meek tone. "Yes, I said that. But only to convince you to free me. Now I am terribly hungry," said the lion.

The terrified man thought quickly. He said, "Alright, you can eat me. But let a judge decide if you are right in eating the person who has rescued you."

The lion agreed. He was sure that no animal would speak against him. Just then a jackal came that way and the lion asked him to be the judge. The jackal was cunning like all jackals. He addressed the lion, "Sir, would you please show me how it all happened?" The lion was only too willing. He entered the cage and closed the cage door. The jackal immediately bolted the cage from outside.

"Now the lion is trapped again. Run away, you foolish man! And never offer help to anyone without thinking," said the jackal. The frightened man ran for his life. And the ungrateful lion was trapped in the cage again. The hunter came and took him away.

The Greedy Dog

Once, there lived a dog. He was very greedy. There were many times that he had to pay for his greed. Each time the dog promised himself, "I have learnt my lesson. Now I will never be greedy again." But he soon forgot his promises and was as greedy as ever.

One afternoon, the dog was terribly hungry. He decided to go and look for something to eat. Just outside his house there was a bridge. "I'll go and look for food on the other side of the bridge. The food there is definitely better," he thought to himself.

He walked across the wooden bridge and started sniffing around for food. Suddenly, he spotted a bone lying at a distance. "Ah, I am in luck. This looks like a delicious bone," he said.

Without wasting any time, the hungry dog picked up the bone and was just about to eat it, when he thought, "Somebody

might see me here with this bone and then I'll have to share it. I'd better go home and eat it." Holding the bone in his mouth he ran towards his house.

While crossing the wooden bridge, the dog looked down into the river. He saw his own reflection. The foolish dog mistook it for another dog. "There is another dog in the water with a bone," he thought. Greedy, as he was, he thought, "How nice it would be to snatch that piece of bone as well. Then, I will have two bones."

So, the dog looked at his reflection and growled. The reflection growled back, too. This made the dog angry. He looked down at his reflection and barked, "Woof! Woof!" As he opened his mouth, the bone fell into the river. It was only when the water splashed that the greedy dog realised that what he had seen was his own reflection and not another dog. But it was too late. He had lost the piece of bone because of his greed. Now he had to go hungry.

The Bullock's Curse

Long time ago, in a small village lived an old woman with her daughter. While the old woman was hard-working, her daughter was lazy and selfish. They had a bullock. "We should take proper care of our bullock," the old woman would say. "Hah! Animals should serve us, not we serve them," the daughter would reply.

There was a pond, some distance from the old woman's house. Every afternoon she used to take the bullock to the pond to have a bath and drink water. Meanwhile, the lazy daughter would eat and sleep.

One day, the old woman fell ill. She requested her daughter to take the bullock to the pond. "It's very hot today, dear! The bullock must be thirsty," said the old woman. "Look! I have some sweets here. I know you love sweets, dear. Take the bullock for a drink. While he is drinking water, you can eat these sweets," the old

woman added, handing a box of sweets to her daughter. The greedy girl agreed.

But as soon as she was out of her mother's sight, the lazy girl tied the bullock to a tree and sat down to eat the sweets. The thirsty bullock waited for the daughter to finish eating the sweets. "I hope she eats fast. I am really thirsty," thought the bullock. But after having eaten all the sweets the daughter returned home and lied to her mother that she had taken the bullock to the pond.

The bullock was extremely angry. He cursed the daughter, "In your next birth, may you be born a 'Chatak', a bird that drinks water only when it rains. As you kept me thirsty today, so will you remain thirsty."

The bullock's curse came true. In her next birth, the daughter was born a 'Chatak'. It is said that a 'Chatak' is a bird that waits for rains, remaining thirsty throughout the year, despite having water all around.

The Golden Egg

Haria, a poor barber lived alone in his small hut. He was dedicated to his work and whatever he earned was enough to fulfil his needs.

One evening, after returning from work, Haria was hungry, "What shall I cook tonight?" he thought. Just then he heard a hen clucking outside his hut. "That hen would make a great feast," thought Haria and prepared to catch the hen.

With a little effort he was able to catch the hen. As he was about to kill the hen, it squeaked, "Please don't kill me, O kind man! I will help you." Haria stopped. Though he was surprised that the hen spoke, he asked, "How can you help me?"

"If you spare my life, I will lay a golden egg everyday for you," said the hen. Haria's eyes widened in delight. "A Golden egg! But why should I believe you? You might be lying," said Haria. "If I don't lay a golden

egg tomorrow, you can kill me," said the hen.

The next morning, Haria found a golden egg lying outside his hut and the hen sitting beside it. "It's true! You really can lay a golden egg!" exclaimed Haria with great delight.

From that day, the hen would lay a golden egg everyday. In return, Haria took good care of the hen. Very soon, Haria became rich.

But he became greedy. He thought, "If I cut open the hen's stomach, I can get out all the golden eggs at once. I don't have to wait for the hen to lay the eggs one by one."

That night Haria killed the hen. But to his dismay, he found no golden eggs. Not even one.

"What have I done? My greed has made me kill the hen," he wailed. But it was too late.

The Prince And The Snake

The kingdom of Vijaygarh had a wise and kind King. People were happy. But the King himself was sad and worried. A devilish snake had entered his son's body. Neither medicine worked nor magic.

When the Prince grew up he thought, "It's because of me that my father is worried." And one day, he left the palace. Wandering, he came to another kingdom. He found a desolate temple and started living there. He begged for food.

The King of that land was cruel. But he had a kind and beautiful daughter. The King was unhappy with his daughter, "She is always talking to me of hard work. I must marry her off to a beggar. Then she will know what hard work is," thought the King.

So, when the Prince came to beg for food, the cruel King forced him to marry his daughter. The Prince and his new bride started for the desolate temple. On their

way, they stopped to rest. The Princess went around in search of food, while her husband went to sleep.

When the Princess came back, she was shocked to see a snake sitting on her husband's mouth. On a mound nearby, sat another snake. They were talking. "Why don't you leave the body of the Prince? He is so kind and gentle," said the snake sitting on the mound. "You too are evil! You attack passers-by. You should not be telling me what to do," replied the snake sitting on the Prince's mouth.

The Princess killed the two snakes. When her husband woke up, she told him about the two snakes. The Prince was happy. He told her who he really was. They set off to the Prince's kingdom. The King was delighted to see his son. When the King learnt that the devilish snake had been killed, His joy knew no bounds. The Prince and the Princess lived happily for a long time.

The Cunning Bats

Many years ago, the members of the jungle did not have any king. The animals said, "The lion must be the king of the jungle." While the birds said, "The hawk must be king." There were many discussions and debates, but no final decision could be taken.

The bats were cunning. They approached the animals and said, "Since we too are animals, we would like our dear lion to be king. He is surely the most powerful among us." And the animals thought that the bats were on their side.

The bats then went to the birds. "Since we are birds, our dear hawk must be made king. He is so royal and dignified," they said. And the birds thought that the bats were on their side.

A few days went by. One day the birds came to know that the cunning bats were not honest. They informed the animals

about this. "So the bats think they are clever, let us teach them a lesson," said the animals.

So, the next day, the birds and the animals made peace with each other. The lion was made the king. The newly crowned king addressed to the bats, "You must choose the group to which you belong." The bats thought, "We must join the animals because the lion is the king."

"We are animals!" the bats announced. "But you have wings. No animal has wings. You must join the birds," said all the animals. "Bats have babies. They don't lay eggs. And birds lay eggs. The bats can't be birds," said the birds. The bats felt helpless. They just stood there, not knowing what to do.

Since then, the bats have been hiding during the daytime in deserted places. They come out for food only at night when others are asleep.

The Fragrance

In a small town lived a wealthy merchant. He was very kind and charitable. He had a son, who had unfortunately fallen into bad company. Many times the merchant advised his son. But all in vain. "Please do not advise me, father. I know what is good for me," said the son.

One day, a great saint came to that town. The merchant went to him, sought his blessings and said, "My spoilt son is the only cause of my worry. Please help me." "Send your son to my ashram tomorrow morning. I will talk to him," said the saint.

Next morning, the merchant sent his son to the saint's ashram. There the saint asked him to pluck a rose from the garden. "Smell it and feel its fragrance, my son," said the saint. The boy did so. Then the saint showed him a sack of wheat and said, "Keep the rose near this sack." The boy followed the instruction.

After an hour the saint asked him to smell the rose again. "How does it smell now?" the saint asked. The boy smelt the rose and said, "It smells as good as before." "Hmm! Now keep the rose near this sack of jaggery," said the saint.

After another hour, the saint asked the boy to smell the rose again. "Is there any change in the fragrance?" the saint asked. "No, it smells as fresh as before," replied the boy.

Then the saint said, "Boy, you should be like this rose, giving fragrance to everyone but at the same time not letting the bad smell rub on to you from anyone. Your good qualities are your strength. You should not lose them in bad company."

The boy understood the saint's words and wisdom. "I am grateful to you, O Saint, for opening my eyes," said the merchant's son. From that day, he was honest and charitable like his father.

The Magic Pot

One hot afternoon, Gopi, a poor farmer was digging his field. All of a sudden, his spade hit something. "It is a big metal pot," said Gopi. It was big enough to boil rice for a hundred people. "It doesn't seem to be of any use to me. I will dig deeper. May be I'll find something else," thought Gopi. He continued to dig.

After he had dug for a long time, Gopi felt tired. "It's of no use. There is nothing in this field," he thought. He threw his spade into the pot in frustration and sat under a tree to rest.

After a while, when he got up to leave, he could not believe his eyes. There were one hundred spades in the pot. "This is a magical pot. I will put this mango inside the pot and see what happens," Gopi thought. Gopi put a mango into the pot. To his amazement, he found one hundred mangoes in the pot. Gopi carried the pot home.

With the magic pot Gopi became a rich man. The King came to know of the magic pot. He was a curious and greedy King. "I want to find out the secret of the magic pot. If it is so valuable it has to be in the King's treasury," said the King. The King ordered his men to bring the magic pot.

When the magic pot was brought to the King, he did not know what to do. The King thought, "Let me see what is there inside this pot that makes it magical." He peered inside. He slipped and fell into the pot. When he climbed out, he was shocked to see one hundred Kings.

All the Kings now started claiming the throne. They fought among themselves and died. The magic pot lay in the King's treasury. "The foolish King took away the magic pot from me because of his curiosity. Now it has killed him," thought Gopi, sadly.

The Ignorant Man

Deenu was a milkman. He had built his hut far away from the village, in the woods. He loved the quiet of the woods rather than the noise of the village. He lived there with his two cows. He fed them well and took proper care of them. With the milk that the cows gave, he earned enough money to live happily.

Deenu was an honest man. Though he was content, at times he would be restless. "There is so much wrong and evil in this world. Is there nobody to guide the people?" this thought made him sad.

One evening, Deenu was returning home after selling milk in the village. He saw a saint sitting under a tree and meditating. He slowly walked up to him and waited for the saint to open his eyes.

After a while, the saint opened his eyes. He was surprised to see a man patiently sitting beside him. "What do you want?"

asked the saint humbly. "I want to know what is the path to Truth and Piety. Where shall I find Honesty?" asked Deenu.

The saint smiled and said, "Go to the pond nearby and ask the fish the same question. She will give you the answer."

Deenu went to the pond and asked the same question to the fish. The fish said, "O kind man! First, bring me some water to drink." Deenu was surprised. He said, "You live in water. But you still want water to drink? How strange!"

At this the fish said, "You are right. And that gives you the answer to your question as well. Truth, Piety and Honesty are inside the heart of a man. But being ignorant he searches for them in the outer world. Instead of wandering here and there look within yourself and you would find them."

Deenu thanked the fish and walked home a wiser man. From that day, Deenu never felt restless.

The Dangerous Helper

In a dense forest, there was a lake. In this lake there lived a crab. The crab's best friend was a swan, who lived nearby. They were happy until one day a snake made its home near the lake.

Every time the swan laid an egg, the snake would come and eat it up. "I have to find a way to save my eggs," thought the swan.

One day, he went to the crab and said, "Please help me, dear friend. My eggs are under threat. That cruel snake eats all the eggs in my nest. What can I do?"

The crab thought for a while. Then he said, "I have an idea. Let's catch some fish from this lake and scatter them from the snake's house till the mongoose's house." The crab and the swan caught some fish and dropped them from the mongoose's house all the way to the snake's house. Then both of them hid behind a tree and watched.

After sometime, the mongoose came out. He saw the fish and was overjoyed. "Mmm! Fish right outside my home!" he said, smacking his lips. He ate them one by one. As he ate he kept following the fish trail to the snake's house. Finally, he reached the snake's house.

When the snake saw the mongoose, he thought, "That mongoose is here to attack me. I better fight." After a fierce battle, the mongoose killed the snake.

The swan heaved a sigh of relief. But her joy was short-lived. The next day, the mongoose, looking for more fish came upon the swan's eggs. He immediately ate them. The swan and the crab now felt helpless. They had brought this new threat upon themselves. "Our thoughtless act has got us a new enemy. Even more dangerous than the previous one," cried the two friends.

The Stubborn Hunter

Once upon a time, there lived a hunter. He loved hunting rabbits. He liked rabbit meat.

Many a time he was advised by his friends to give up hunting. "You should stop being so cruel," said his friends. "I know what I am doing. Please don't advise me," shouted the hunter, annoyed.

One sunny afternoon, the hunter was busy preparing to go on another hunting expedition. Just then a saint happened to pass by. Seeing the hunter holding a rope, a spear, a knife and a net, the saint said, "It seems to me you are going to catch an animal." "Yes, I am going to catch a rabbit," replied the hunter.

"But what will you do with that rabbit?" asked the saint. "I will cut its throat, roast it and eat it up. Will you stop me?" asked the hunter, irritated with the saint. "No, my son! I only wanted to tell you that killing innocent animals is a sin. All sinners get

punished some day," said the humble saint. The hunter yelled back at the saint, "Let me see who comes to punish me." And he left in anger. The saint smiled and sat there in meditation.

After sometime, the hunter was back. He was holding a rabbit by its ears. "Ha! Ha! See I have caught my prey. Now I will cut its throat and roast it right in front of you. No one will come to punish me," he said to the still meditating saint. Just as the hunter was about to raise his knife, it slipped out of his hand and landed on his foot. "Yieee!" he screamed, letting go of the rabbit. The rabbit ran away.

The hunter's foot was badly cut. He was in pain. But the hunter knew that what had just happened was divine justice. "I have now realised how cruel and stubborn I've been. I will give up hunting completely," said the hunter to the saint. He thanked the saint for the words of wisdom and went on his way.

The Naughty Lamb

Once upon a time, there lived a mother goat and her little lamb. The lamb was very naughty. The mother goat found it difficult to manage him.

The mother goat felt worried. Their home was near the edge of the forest and there were many wolves in the forest.

One day, the lamb wandered into the forest. He enjoyed looking at the tall trees and lovely flowers.

Suddenly he realised he was lost. "Oh my! I have come far away from home. Mother will be angry with me," he thought.

Out of the little lamb's sight, there was a wolf who was watching from behind a tree. "Yummy! That lamb is exactly what I want for lunch today," he thought, licking his lips in anticipation.

The wolf jumped in front of the lamb and, barring his sharp teeth, said, "A little

fellow like you should not be getting into the forest. I am going to eat you."

The little lamb was terrified. He stood still for a moment, then he turned and ran as fast as he could. The wolf followed closely.

Meanwhile, the mother goat not finding her lamb at home was worried. "I hope he has not gone into the forest. I must go and look for him," she thought.

Just as she was about to get into the forest, she saw the little lamb coming out of the forest. He was panting and there was a wolf chasing. The mother goat using her long horns chased the wolf away.

The little lamb was shivering in fear. Mother goat took him home and when he had calmed down, said, "Now, I hope you have learnt your lesson. The forest is no place for goats." The little lamb just nodded.

The Selfish Crows

On a huge banyan tree, there lived many crows. They were very selfish and arrogant. They had no friends, as no one liked them.

When the rainy season came, dark clouds gathered in the sky. A small mynah was returning to her nest. When she was passing the banyan tree it started raining. "I will stay here until it stops raining," thought the mynah, resting on the banyan tree.

The crows saw her perching on the tree. One of them shouted, "Get off the tree. This tree belongs to us." The mynah pleaded, "The weather is bad and my nest is far off. Please let me rest here for a while, brother."

"Leave at once! Or we will peck you," said the other crows. The scared mynah flew off to a nearby tree, where luckily she found a hollow in a broken branch. She took shelter there.

Shortly after, the rain became heavy followed by hailstones. Even the leaves and branches were not enough to shelter the crows. Many of them were hurt by the hailstones. But the mynah was safe inside the hollow.

One of the crows said, "Look at the mynah! How comfortable she is. Let us go there." Another crow said, "I don't think she will let us share the hollow. We did not have sympathy for her when she was in need." Then another crow said, "We shouldn't have been so rude. We forgot that we may need help someday."

Suddenly the mynah called out, "Come to this hollow, friends! Or you will get hurt. The rain is not going to stop soon."

The crows flew down to the hollow. They thanked the mynah, "We are sorry for having been unkind, dear friend! Now we will never be so selfish."

The Donkey And The Horse

Once, there lived a washerman named Bheema. He had a donkey and a horse. The donkey carried clothes to the pond and back home. The horse carried Bheema to the market and back, occasionally. The donkey worked much harder than the horse.

On a bright sunny day, Bheema was going to the pond with his donkey. He took the horse along to give it a drink of water. The donkey was carrying a heavy load of clothes. The horse was carrying nothing. The load was unusually heavy and the donkey's back was hurting.

When the pain became unbearable the donkey said to the horse, "This load is too much for me, brother! Please take some of it on your back." The horse said rudely, "Eh! Why should I? I only carry my master to the market." The proud horse continued on his way. The day was getting hotter. The donkey felt totally exhausted. He was

almost dragging himself. "Humph! Humph!" The donkey tried to move. He just couldn't. The poor donkey collapsed on to the ground. "Oh, what has happened to the poor donkey?" said the washerman.

Immediately, he took the load off the donkey. "Indeed the load is very heavy. I should have been a little more careful," thought the washerman. Then he gave some water to the donkey. The donkey felt better now.

The washerman then picked up the bundle of clothes and 'thump!' He placed it on the horse's back. "Umf! Umf!" came the sound from the horse's mouth. "I should have helped the donkey. I made a mistake. I should have taken half the load when the donkey requested me. Now I realise sharing a burden is easier." The horse carried the heavy clothes a long distance.

In a mango orchard outside a village, there lived a mischievous monkey. The whole day, he would jump from one tree to another, eating the ripe mangoes. The orchard-keeper had tried to trap the monkey. But every time the monkey escaped the trap.

One day, the monkey wandered out to the town, "The town people are so busy. There is so much crowd here," he thought. Soon the monkey was sneaking into houses and running away with the eatables. By evening, he had made life difficult for the town people. "The town is more fun than the orchard. I will live here," he thought.

Days went by and the monkey was looked upon by the town people with terror. "Here he comes again," they screamed, when they saw the monkey.

One day, the juggler came to the town. The people of the town approached him. "We

want you to help us get rid of that monkey," they said. The juggler said, "Don't worry. Get me some jars with narrow necks."

When the jars were brought to him, he put peanuts into the jars and placed them out on a field.

The monkey became curious when he saw the jars. When he went and peeped inside the jars he saw peanuts, "Yummy! Let me quickly grab the peanuts and run," he thought. He put his hand inside the jar and grabbed a big handful.

But he could not pull out his clenched fist, as the neck of the jar was too narrow. If the monkey dropped some peanuts back into the jar, he could have pulled out his hand. But he was greedy.

The town people trapped the monkey with his hand in the jar. They got hold of ropes and tied the monkey. He was sold to a zoo. That was the end of the greedy monkey.

There once lived a salt merchant. He had a donkey. Every morning, he would load a sack of salt on the donkey and go to the nearby town to sell it. On the way they had to walk across a pond.

One day, while crossing the pond the donkey thought, "Ooh! This load is so heavy. I wish I could get some of this load taken off my back." Just then the donkey tripped and fell into the water.

Fortunately, the donkey was not hurt. But the sack of salt on the donkey's back fell into the water. Some of the salt in the sack got dissolved, making the load on the donkey lighter. The donkey felt very happy. The merchant helped him get up and they carried on their journey.

From that day, it became a regular practice for the donkey to slip and fall in the pond. This would dissolve some salt in the sack, relieving the donkey of some load.

The merchant was not aware of the donkey's cunningness. This continued for a few days.

One day, the merchant noticed the donkey deliberately slipping and landing with the sack into the water. "Oh! So this is why I am losing salt everyday," he thought. He decided to teach the donkey a lesson.

Next morning, instead of loading a sack of salt, the merchant loaded a sack of cotton on the donkey's back. While crossing the pond, the donkey, as usual, slipped and fell into the water.

But this time, when he got up, the load on his back seemed heavier. "Ooh! The load seems to have gotten heavier," thought the donkey.

The merchant looked at the donkey and said, "Dear friend, I saw you fall into the water deliberately. So I loaded a sack of cotton. Cotton when wet weighs heavier. Now you will have to carry it to town." The poor donkey had learnt his lesson.

85

The Pigeon And The Bad Crows

Once upon a time, there lived a farmer. Whenever he sowed seeds in his farm, the crows would come and eat them up.

"I must do something about these crows. I will be ruined if I don't stop them," he thought.

The next day, the farmer bought a scarecrow and placed it on the farm. Then he sowed his seeds. "This season, I hope, I'll get a good harvest," he said to himself, softly.

When the farmer came a few days later, he saw that the crows had pushed the scarecrow on to the ground. And the grains were all eaten. The farmer cried out, "I am ruined."

The farmer sat the whole night, thinking of a plan to get rid of the crows. Finally, just before dawn he had an idea, "I must go to the town and buy a large net. I will trap the crows in the net."

The farmer bought a net and some grain. He laid the net on the farm and spread the grain over it. Then he went and hid himself.

Soon the crows were there. "More grain! That farmer is indeed foolish, he does not seem to learn," said the crows to each other and laughed. But suddenly they realised that they were trapped.

Before long, the farmer was standing over the crows. "Aha, finally, I've got you all. For the destruction you have caused me, I'll put you all to death."

Suddenly the farmer heard a feeble voice. There was a pigeon among the crows. The pigeon said, "Mr. Farmer, please let me go. You are angry with the crows not with me."

The farmer said, "But you too have been caught stealing from my farm. I will not spare you," said the farmer. The pigeon had to pay a heavy price for having been in bad company.

The Clever Bull

Once, a bull wandering in the forest came upon a cave. Near the cave was a big pond and lush green grass. "This is an ideal place to settle down," the bull thought. So, he made the cave his home. Many days passed. The bull became quite healthy, grazing in the meadows.

One day, the bull was resting outside his cave. A lion happened to come that way. "Aha! A bull. He is so healthy too," thought the lion, licking his lips in anticipation of a good meal. The bull too noticed the lion. He could sense danger. "I must be on my guard now," he thought.

When the lion came close to the bull, the bull looked into the cave and called out, "Darling, don't cook anything for dinner. I have just spotted a lion. I am waiting for it to come near." When the lion heard the bull, he turned around and ran for his life.

A jackal saw the lion running breathlessly. "Why are you running, Mr. Lion?" asked the jackal. The lion told him all that had happened. "The bull has made a fool out of you," the jackal said, "Come with me. Together we will feast on him." But the lion was too scared to believe the jackal. "Alright then! Tie your tail with mine and let me lead you. In case the bull attacks then I'll be the one to get caught first," the jackal said. The lion agreed. The jackal and the lion tied their tails together. They set off to the bull's cave.

When the bull saw the lion coming with the jackal, he thought, "I am sure that cunning jackal knows I fooled the lion." Without panicking, the bull cried out to the jackal, "I had asked you to bring me two lions. Do you want to keep my children hungry?" The lion did not realise that the bull was fooling him again. He was terrified. He ran as fast as could dragging the jackal with him over stones and thorns. The clever bull outwitted his enemies and saved himself.

The Trees And The Lions

In a jungle, there were thousands of trees. Among them two were very good friends. They stood side by side. The same jungle was the home of some lions. They used to kill other animals and eat them. The carcasses of the dead animals used to stink and a foul smell would hang in the air.

One day, the two trees, who were friends were talking. The first tree said, "These lions are polluting the jungle. They must be driven out of here." "Yes," agreed the other tree. A wise old tree, who was listening to the friends said, "They might be polluting the air but these wild creatures are keeping us safe from woodcutters. No woodcutter will dare to come into the forest with lions."

But the two friends decided to frighten the animals away. That evening, the two trees started shaking violently. "We will frighten the lions away. They will be so terrified that they will leave this jungle and

never come back again," said the two friends and laughed aloud. The whole forest echoed with their laughter. "Don't do that!" shouted the wise tree.

But the two friends did not listen. They began moving in the wind and making eerie noises. All the wild animals in the jungle were scared, seeing the two trees. "There is something happening in this forest. Let's run away," they said. All the animals fled the forest. The two friends were happy. "Huh! Now we can enjoy some fresh air," they said.

But their joy was short-lived. One day a woodcutter came to the forest and started felling the trees. "Now there is no fear of the ferocious lions," he muttered to himself. Soon there were other woodcutters. Seeing this, the wise tree said, "Now we'll all be doomed." The two friends cried out, "How foolish we've been. We should have listened to the wise tree." A little later the two trees were brought down by the woodcutter's axe.

The Bone In Throat

Once upon a time, there was a lazy wolf living in a jungle. Near his house was a pond. Many animals came to the pond to drink water. The wolf was always in search of food.

One day, he was sitting near the pond, hoping to get something to eat, when suddenly he spotted a dead bull. "Aha! What a luck! Now I can eat all I want," he thought and his mouth started watering.

He began to eat the bull. A thought struck him, "If another beast comes this way he will ask for a share. I'd better eat fast." 'Grub! Gulp! Grub! Gulp!' he chewed, faster and faster.

In his haste, a piece of bone got stuck in his throat. "Ohh! Errk!" cried the wolf. He tried to cough it out but in vain. Next, he tried to swallow it down but he failed.

"Ooh, this bone hurts. What shall I do now?" thought the wolf. Suddenly he

remembered that a crane lived on the nearby riverbank.

The wolf went to the crane and pleaded, "My dear Crane"! I've got a bone stuck in my throat. I will give you a present if you pull it out with your long beak."

The crane took pity on the wolf. He asked the wolf to look up with his mouth open. The crane then put its head into the wolf's mouth and pulled out the bone. "Oh! What a relief!" The wolf sighed.

"Now where is my present?" asked the crane. "What present?" the wolf said. "You said you would give me a present if I remove the bone out of your throat," the crane said.

"Hah! Is it not a present that you put your head into my mouth and got out alive? I could have easily crushed your head while your beak was inside my mouth," said the ungrateful wolf and went away.

The Arrogant Swans

In a far away kingdom there was a river. This river was the home to many golden swans. The swans spent most of their time on the banks of the river. Every six months the swans would leave a golden feather as a fee for using the lake. The soldiers of the King would collect the feathers and deposit it in the royal treasury.

One day, a homeless bird saw the river, "The water in this river seems so cool and soothing. I will make my home here," thought the bird. As soon as the bird settled down near the river, the golden swans noticed her. They came shouting, "This river belongs to us. We pay a golden feather to use this river. You cannot live here."

"I am homeless, brothers! I too will pay the rent. Please give me shelter," the bird pleaded. "How will you pay the rent? You don't have golden feathers," said the swans laughing, "Stop dreaming and leave at

once." The humble bird pleaded many times but the arrogant swans drove her away. "I shall teach them a lesson!" thought the humiliated bird. She went to the King and said, "O King! The swans in your river are impolite and unkind. I begged for shelter but they said that they had purchased the river with golden feathers."

The King was angry with the swans for having insulted the homeless bird. He ordered his soldiers to bring the arrogant swans to his court. In no time, all the golden swans were brought to the King's court.

"Do you think the royal treasury depends upon your golden feathers? You cannot decide who lives by the river. Leave the river at once or you all will be beheaded!" shouted the King.

The swans shivered with fear on hearing the King. They flew away never to return. The bird built her home near the river and lived there happily.

The Palace And The Hut

King Vikramaditya was known for his justice and kindness. Even Gods sought his help in settling issues. In his kingdom, no one was unhappy. His people loved him and were proud of him.

Once King Vikramaditya decided to build a palace on the riverbank. He ordered his minister to survey the site and start the work. The labourers were put to work and in a few days the palace was ready. Before bringing the King to show the palace, the minister decided to take a final look.

"Splendid!" the minister exclaimed, looking at the palace. Then suddenly his eyes fell on something and he shouted, "Whhhat's that? I didn't see that before." All the labourers and the soldiers turned around. There was a hut just a few steps away from the palace gate. "What is this hut doing here?" shouted the minister, "And whom does it belong to?" "Sir, it belongs to

an old woman. She has been living here for a long time," replied a soldier.

The minister walked up to the hut and spoke to the old lady. "I want to buy your hut. Ask for anything," he said. "I am sorry, Sir. I cannot accept your offer. My hut is more dear to me than my life. I have lived in it with my late husband and I want to die in it," the old lady said. The minister tried to tell her that her hut would spoil the charm of the newly constructed palace. But the old lady was ready to face any punishment rather than sell the hut. The matter was then taken to the King.

The wise and generous King thought for a while, then said, "Let the old lady have her hut where it is. It will only add to the beauty of my palace." Then turning to the minister, the King said, "Let us not forget that what seems ugly to us may be precious to someone else." The people then realised why their King was so highly respected.

The Iron Box

Mohan Das was the son of a rich businessman. When his father died, he left Mohan Das an iron box with valuables in it. One day, Mohan Das had to go to the city on some work. So, he took the iron box and handed it over to his moneylender friend, Ramasewak. "Please keep this box. My father gave it to me. I will return from the city and collect it from you," said Mohan Das. "You don't have to worry. I will keep this box safely," said Ramasewak.

Mohan Das started off happily. He knew that his valuable iron box was safe with Ramasewak. A few days later he returned. He went to his friend Ramasewak and asked for the iron box. Ramasewak pretended to look a little surprised, "Oh, the iron box! The rats ate it up. I just couldn't stop them," he said.

Mohan Das realised that his friend had become greedy and dishonest. Ramasewak was trying to cheat him. Being an intelligent

man, he kept quiet. "I must figure out a way to get my box back," thought Mohan Das.

Next day, Mohan Das went to Ramasewak and said, "Friend! Can you send your son with me? I need someone to look after my property." "Mohan Das seems to be a fool. May be he will reward my son well for looking after his property," thought Ramasewak. He agreed and sent his son with Mohan Das.

Next morning, Mohan Das came running to Ramasewak and said, "Dear friend, a terrible thing has happened. A hawk has carried your son away." Ramasewak was furious, he cried out, "But how can a hawk carry off a boy?" "In the same way as the rats can eat up an iron box," replied Mohan Das, with a slight smile. "I am sorry, friend! I realise my mistake," said Ramasewak. He felt ashamed for having tried to cheat his friend. He gave the iron box back to Mohan Das.

Foolish Imitation

Long ago, a hawk lived on the top of a hill. At the foot of the hill there was a banyan tree on which a crow used to perch everyday. The crow was very foolish. He would imitate everyone.

The hawk atop the hill would fly down everyday in search of food. The crow watched the hawk circling in the air for long hours and swooping down when he saw his prey. The hawk gifted with eyes that could see long distances would spot his prey from the hilltop and then fly down to pounce upon it.

The crow watched the hawk thinking, "Hunh! If the hawk can do that, I can too. What does he think? One day I will show the hawk I can do the same thing."

A few days later, as the hawk was circling in the air, the crow decided to do the same. Suddenly a baby rabbit came out

of the bushes. The hawk saw it and so did the crow.

Before the crow could move, the hawk swooped down, caught hold of the rabbit in his strong sharp talons and flew away. 'Swooosh!' was all the crow heard as the hawk disappeared in the sky with his prey. "Hmmph! That is no great skill," thought the crow, angrily.

Next moment he spotted a big fat mouse coming out of a hole. Without wasting time, the crow swooped down. Like the hawk he tried to catch the mouse in his claws.

But the mouse saw the crow and moved away, the crow crashed against the hill. "Eeeaaa!" cried the crow in pain.

Just then the hawk came flying down, "I hope, now you know it is not easy to hunt and it's not easy to imitate, either," said the hawk and flew away.

On a mango tree in a jungle, there lived many birds. They were happy in their small nests. Before the onset of the rainy season, all the animals of the jungle repaired their homes. The birds also made their homes more secure.

Some of the birds brought twigs and leaves and the others wove the nests. "We should also store some food for our children," chirped one of the birds. And they collected food, until they had enough to see them through the rainy season. They kept themselves busy preparing for the tough times.

Soon the rains came. It was followed by thunder and lightning. All the animals and birds stayed in their homes.

It continued raining for many days. One day, a monkey wet in the rain came into the forest. He sat on a branch, shivering with cold, water dripping from his body.

The poor monkey tried his best to get shelter. But in vain. The leaves were not enough to save him from the rains. "Brrr! It's so cold!" said the monkey.

The birds were watching all this. They felt sorry for the monkey but there was little they could do for him. One of them said, "Brother! Our small nests are not enough to give you shelter."

Another bird said, "All of us prepared for the rainy season. If you had, you wouldn't be in this situation."

"How dare you tell me what to do?" said the monkey, growling at the bird. The monkey angrily pounced on the bird's nest, tore it and threw it on the ground. The bird and her chicks were helpless.

The poor bird thought, "Fools never value good advice. It is better not to advise them."

The Lamb And The Wolf

Once there was a naughty lamb. His mother always warned him, "Be careful! You must not go into the forest. Wild animals live in there." But the mischievous lamb never listened.

One day, the lamb wandered off into the forest. There he saw a spring, "I am thirsty. Let me drink some water," he thought. While the lamb was drinking water a wolf watched from behind a tree.

"A lamb! My lucky day!" the wolf thought, approaching the lamb. "You know this forest belongs only to wild animals. Why have you come in here?" asked the wolf.

The lamb knew that wolves were dangerous animals. "Mother has warned me about wolves. I am sure this fellow wants to eat me. I must escape," he thought.

The wolf continued, "You are also dirtying the water. How will I drink it now?"

"But the spring flows from where you are standing down to where I am, Sir!" said the lamb, in a meek voice.

The wolf was just looking for an excuse to kill the lamb. "How dare you argue with me? I think you are the same lamb who had abused me last year," the wolf shouted. "Last year?? But Sir, I was not even born then!" the lamb squeaked.

The lamb heard some woodcutters coming their way. "If I can keep talking to this wolf for a little while longer, the woodcutters will be here. They will chase him away," thought the clever lamb. So, he said, "Mr. Wolf, you are right. I have dirtied the water. But I did not mean to upset you." As the lamb spoke, the woodcutters arrived.

They caught the wolf and beat him before letting him go. The lamb was relieved to be safe. He ran back to his mother, promising never to wander into the forest again.

There once lived a proud stag. While wandering in the forest he came upon a pond. He stopped there to drink water. As he bent down, he saw his reflection in the water. "How beautiful are my antlers!" he thought, admiring its long curves.

As the stag was admiring his antlers, he suddenly noticed his legs. "Ohh! Look at my skinny legs. I cannot believe God has given me both beautiful antlers and such ugly legs," he thought. The proud stag now felt ashamed of his legs. His pride vanished. "These ugly legs are no match for my beautiful antlers," he thought.

Just then the stag heard the roar of a lion. When he turned around he saw a lion charging at him. "Oh no!" screamed the stag and ran as fast as he could.

The stag felt the lion's breath close to him, "I must get into the densest part of the forest where there are many branches.

The lion will not be able to catch me in there," thought the stag.

So, with this thought in mind, the stag ran into an area where there were many bushes and branches. Soon the stag had left the lion far behind.

"Ah, I outsmarted the lion," thought the stag, proudly. But all of a sudden his antlers got entangled between the trunks of two trees standing close to each other. "Aaarghh!" cried the stag, as he had to stop at once.

The more he tried to free himself the more difficult it became. As the stag was struggling to get free, the lion came nearer and nearer.

"How I praised my horns and cursed my legs. Now I know the real value of my legs which almost took me to safety," wailed the stag.

The lion pounced on the stag and killed him. That was the end of the proud stag.

The Donkey And The Dog

A washerman had a donkey and a dog. One night, some thieves broke into the washerman's house. The dog heard them and started barking. The washerman got up and so did the neighbours. "What's that! A dog. Let's run," said the thieves. They tried to run but were caught.

The washerman said, "I am glad I had this dog in my house. I am sure the thieves would have looted me if my dog had not barked." Everyone too praised the dog.

From that day, the donkey started thinking, "The master thinks the dog is a more useful animal than me." The donkey decided he will show his master, the washerman, that he too could be useful just like the dog. Some days passed. One night, it so happened, two thieves again entered the washerman's house. "We should be careful, friend! I have heard that a dog guards the house," one thief said to the other.

As the thieves peeped in, they saw the dog sitting just outside the main door. "It seems the dog is quite alert," said one thief. "It is better to leave this house alone," the other thief said and the two thieves fled. But unknown to the thieves, the donkey was watching all this. He thought, "It's a good opportunity for me to show my master that I can be useful, too. The thieves have run away. If I start shouting the master will think I have driven them out." And the foolish donkey started braying loudly.

When the washerman heard the donkey bray at this odd hour, he got angry. He came out with a stick and thrashed the donkey. "This will teach him not to bray at night," he screamed.

Just then the dog came to the donkey and said, "It is better to do your duties than try to be like me." The donkey knew, the dog was right.

The Clever Fox

There once lived a crow. One day he was very hungry. He had not been able to get any food the previous day. "If I don't get anything to eat I'll starve to death," he thought.

As the crow was searching for food, his eyes fell on a piece of bread. He quickly swooped down, picked it up and flew off. Far away in a lonely place he sat on a tree to enjoy the bread.

Just then a hungry fox saw the crow sitting on the tree holding the bread in its mouth. "Yummy! That bread looks delicious. What I would give to get that piece of bread," the fox thought.

The fox decided to use all his cunning means to get the piece of bread from the crow. He sat under the tree. The crow saw him and thought, "I guess this fox wants to eat my bread. I shall hold it carefully." And he held on to the bread even more tightly.

The clever fox spoke to the crow politely. He said, "Hello friend! How are you?" But the crow did not say anything. "Crows are such lovely birds. And you are very charming too," said the fox, flattering the crow.

Then the fox said, "I have heard that besides being beautiful you also have a sweet voice. Please sing a song for me."

By now the crow started to believe what the fox was saying. "The fox knows true beauty. I must be the most beautiful bird in this whole world. I will sing him a song," thought the crow.

As soon as the foolish crow opened his mouth to sing, the bread fell from his beak. The fox, who had just been waiting for this very moment, caught the bread in his mouth and gulped it down his throat.

The crow had paid a heavy price for his foolishness.

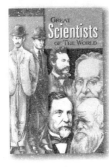
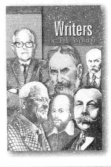

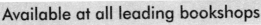

Biography Series 8 Titles   Rs.15/- *each*

M. K. GANDHI

MOTHER TERESA

RABINDRANATH TAGORE

WILLIAM SHAKESPEARE

NELSON MANDELA

J.R.D. TATA

ABRAHAM LINCOLN

ASHOKA

SPIDER BOOKS

▶ Available at all leading bookshops ◀